Hotwife Blind Date - A Steamy Romance Hot Wife Novel

Karly Violet

Published by Karly Violet, 2020.

Hotwife Blind Date
A Steamy Romance Hot Wife Novel

This is a work of fiction. Similarities to real people, places, or events are entirely coincidental.

HOTWIFE BLIND DATE - A STEAMY ROMANCE HOT WIFE NOVEL

First edition. October 12, 2020.

Copyright © 2020 Karly Violet.

ISBN: 979-8201736071

Written by Karly Violet.

Sign up to my Patreon account and receive exclusive Hotwife stories every month and sexy scenes every week!

https://www.patreon.com/karlyviolet

Chapter One: Who's Your Date?

"Okay, we're on in ten, people," a voice announces through speakers in the studio. "Let's get everything ready to go."

I turn to look at the host of the show, Lawson Turner, and smile. "Here we go again, huh?"

"Yeah, show two-forty-nine." I have worked with the middle-aged television personality for the last three years on *Who's Your Date,* and it has been a whirlwind of success for us as well as the television network for which we have been filming.

"Let's go give the old pep talk, alright?" I wave Lawson toward one side of the stage where a young man is sitting in a chair. The makeup artist is applying the last touch of makeup to his young face as we approach. "Charlie, we have met already, but I'm Brandon Knighten, the director and executive producer of the show and this is the show's host, Lawson Turner."

He reaches out and shakes our hands. "Yeah, I remember you." Swallowing hard, he continues, "This is surreal, you know? I'm about to be on live television and I just hope I don't puke all over the stage."

Lawson chuckles as he looks nervously at the man. We have had a few others to vomit on stage before, but most of the time that has happened during commercials or just before the show. "Just take deep breaths when you can, alright? The questions are on the cue cards in your hands."

Charlie looks down at the index cards in his hands. "I didn't think that you guys would actually let me ask my own questions."

"We always let our men ask their questions, so long as they are the sort of questions that won't get us in trouble with the FCC or the studio executives. Of course, we tweak them a little to make them a bit more palatable to the audience," I tell him. "You need to stick to those questions as well as to comments that aren't offensive in general. We are going to be live on the east coast, but thankfully we will be able to edit anything that hops out unexpectedly for the rest of the country." It is my hope that Charlie will take this as a calming thought since he will not be live before the entire country all at once.

He nods his head. "I'll try to keep what I say a little cleaner than usual."

"Four minutes," the same voice from earlier suddenly says from the speakers mounted high on the walls.

"Well, here we go." I smile at the young man before turning to walk with Lawson back toward his position on the stage.

The host shakes his head as we approach a podium. "I'm not sure he can make it through, Brandon. That kid is looking a little too green."

I pat the older man on the shoulder. "He'll be just fine. Once things are rolling along, Charlie will fall right into the role and find a young woman for a nice date."

Lawson smiles. "He pukes. I have ten bucks on that. And it won't be during a commercial, Brandon. That kid is going to pop while on stage."

Raising an eyebrow, I reach out to shake the host's hand. "You're on. I'll expect that ten note on my desk by the end of the day."

"And I'll expect it in my pocket before then as well." Lawson has been a host on television of one sort or another for the last twenty years. He is good at his job and has an uncanny knack to read others and to direct a program toward a ratings-winning conclusion. It is because of this fact that I suddenly wish I had not taken him up on the bet.

"One minute." I nod my head as I look at the row of windows behind the audience seating high up in the studio. Though I am the show's director, I tend to stay out of the control room during the actual filming of the program. It helps me to be more on top of whatever is happening with our young man and the three women he will be choosing from for his date.

"Five, four, three, two, one..." I drop my hand to give the signal to the three camera operators in the studio to begin filming. The light on each camera turns from red to green and Lawson begins to speak to one of them.

"Good afternoon, America. I'm Lawson Turner, your host on *Who's Your Date?*" The audience clap their hands as a sign with the word

APPLAUSE lights up to let them know to do so. "We have a wonderful young man with us for today's episode. Let's bring him out." Again, the audience applauds and Charlie walks out to take a seat on one side of the stage. There is a partition between him and where three other chairs are situated. He smiles uneasily as he sits up straight and waits for his cue from Lawson. "Tell us about yourself, Charlie."

He swallows hard and for a moment appears as if he might become ill. However, he soon recovers and says, "My name is Charlie Greyson and I'm twenty-four years old. I'm a business accountant with Laughton & Milford in Los Angeles and I'm up for a promotion soon." He smiles widely as the audience claps their hands for a third time.

"Very nice," Lawson says as he looks over at the other side of the stage. "Let's bring out our lovely young ladies for this afternoon. Charlie, please say hello to Stacy, Megan, and Kimberly." The audience applauds again as the sign lights up above their heads. The three young women walk toward the three chairs on the other side of the partition from where Charlie is currently seated. He cannot see them and they cannot see him, which is the entire pretense of the show itself. The young man will be selecting which young woman he will take out on a date, all expenses paid by the studio, so that we can follow them around with a camera to find out if true love develops. It is not an entirely new concept on television, but one that I think we have perfected to a point.

"Hello, ladies," Charlie says with a smile on his face. He still appears to be a little sick to his stomach as he moves around uneasily in his seat.

"Ladies, introduce yourselves," Lawson says with a smile.

"My name is Stacy and I am a nice girl originally from the great state of Texas. Hello, Charlie." Her southern voice is sexy as she smiles widely. Stacy is the sort of young woman any guy would love to have as a girlfriend. The tall, blonde beauty would disappoint no man if he were to select her for his date.

"My name is Megan," the second woman says almost immediately afterward. "You should pick me, Charlie. I know how to make a guy's hair stand on end."

"Oh, wow," the young man replies with a nervous chuckle after the cute little brunette introduces herself.

"And I'm Kimberly, Charlie. You can call me Kim if you prefer. I can't wait for our date." Though obviously a little more shy than the other two women, Kimberly appears ready to pick herself for the young man on the other side of the partition.

"Hello," Charlie says as he reaches for a cup of water. He drinks a little but then leans forward as something else happens. Looking first at me nervously, he suddenly puts the cup down on the small table next to his chair. Lawson turns to look at me, a crooked smile on his face.

"Fuck," I mutter to myself as I realize the young man probably vomited a little into the cup. Though it did not happen all over the stage as the host had expected, it is nonetheless a puking event. I owe him ten bucks.

"So, Charlie, let's start with Stacy first. What is your first question." Lawson decides to keep things going so as to not allow the live or television audiences to know what is going on.

He pats his mouth with his hand for a moment before looking at the card in his shaky hand. "Stacy, where would you want to go on a date if I were to select you?"

The young blonde smiles as if she expected the question. Of course, she should have expected it. The show is popular and women all over the country watch it. Stacy likely caught several episodes of it, especially after learning that we might want to put her on as one of the women.

"I would love to go horseback riding. It's been a while since I have gone riding and I miss it a little. Plus, there's the added benefit of the gentle up and down on the horse's back that I really like." She pauses for just a moment before adding, "I really like to be on top while moving up and down slowly, Charlie." There is some sexual tension in the air that is quickly picked up by the audience as they *oooooohhh* at the response.

"Um, that sounds nice," he says as his face turns bright red through the makeup on his cheeks. Moving on to the next young woman, he asks, "Megan, what would you want to do for a first date?"

She looks at Stacy and shakes her head before answering, "You know, horses are nice, but I really like the beach. Volleyball is the best and maybe we could get a game going there. I have lots of sorority sisters from my college days who love to wear two-piece bikinis and hop around on the sand. What do you think, Charlie? Would you like me to bring a dozen of my friends and hop around with you while the sun sets?"

"I would love that," he chuckles as he looks out at the audience. Again, they obviously feel the tension as they root for option number two.

"Wow, is it hot in here, or what?" Lawson jokes as he looks at the camera. "Alright, then; it's time for a question for Kimberly."

"Yeah, Kim," Charlie says as if he had forgotten her momentarily while thinking about the other women. "What would you like to do on a first date with me?"

She nods her head and sits quietly for a moment. Then, as she looks at the partition, she tells him, "Well, I could give you some answer that is full of sexual innuendo, but let's cut the crap, okay?" My heart pounds hard as I worry that Kimberly is about to launch into something that will cause a stern letter from the FCC for this episode. "Let's go have dinner, catch a movie, and then go to a hotel and have sex. Does that sound like a plan, Charlie?"

Suddenly, the young man shakes his head as he looks toward Lawson and gets up from his chair. He runs toward the edge of the stage and vomits just out of sight of the cameras and most of the studio audience. "We will be right back with Charlie's answer right after these messages," the host says with a smile just before the cameras go into standby.

"Dammit," I say under my breath as I walk up to Lawson. Reaching into my pocket, I find a ten-dollar bill and then slide it into his jacket pocket. "I didn't think he would actually get up and run out like that."

"It'll be fine," the host laughs. "He's got the jitters right now and the women today are pouring it on thick. We've been through this all before."

"Yeah, I know, but this guy needs to hold it together for another twenty minutes. If he doesn't, we will have a dud show again, and you know how the executives feel about having one of those."

He shakes his head. "It's not a *dud,* Brandon. Not yet. Give Charlie time to get himself together." Lawson looks up and smiles. "See? He's good as new." I turn to see the young man take his seat on the stage once again before he shuffles the index cards in his hands. Though a little pale, he seems ready to continue. Once the commercial break is over, we do just that and in about twenty more minutes Charlie has chosen Stacy as his date. The audience is happy with the outcome as is the young couple to be. For me, I am just glad that the vomit problem did not literally spill into the show. I can count another one in the books. My day is at an end.

Chapter Two: A Greater Calling

Lila smiles at me as I sit back in my seat at the restaurant. I picked her up from her real estate office after work and took her to get something for dinner. Spending time with the love of my life means everything to me as I relax and look into her eyes.

"It was a good show," she tells me after taking a drink of her wine. "He seemed nervous, but it all ended on a good note, right?"

"A good note," I chuckle. "At least Charlie didn't throw up all over Stacy at the end of the show. That would have been a terrible ending." We both laugh for a moment as I cross my arms and shake my head. "Even though he did that, the guy had the audacity to ask me whether we would film sex between them while on their date."

"What?" Lila's eyes become wide as she giggles. "Did he seriously expect that your cameraman would film that part of their date? Besides, what if the lady didn't want to have sex with him?"

I shrug my shoulders. "He puked but he still felt really confident about sealing the deal," I reply. "Charlie is one of the strangest picks we have had for the male spot in a long time."

"I'll bet." My wife takes another sip of her wine before returning the glass to the table. "So, I sold a nice home today."

"A nice home? You're always selling *nice* homes," I say to her.

"Three million dollars cash," Lila replies. "They took it almost sight-unseen, Brandon. It shocked the hell out of me, but my cut is one hundred thousand dollars."

"Shit." I feel my body quiver a little as I consider the large payout she is getting for her work. "You are really working your clients over, aren't you?"

"I try," Lila says with a smile. "You know how the market in Los Angeles can be, though. Sometimes the market is hot and sometimes it's not so hot. Luckily for me, the market has been on fire for the last three months. I think I will easily double last year's income for this year."

"Damn, honey." Shaking my head, I tell her, "You had better plan on making Christmas really special for me this year."

"Oh, really?" Lila raises an eyebrow while giggling. We have a real chemistry between us that has made up the backbone of our marriage for the last ten years. I love my wife and she loves me. What more could we really ask for?

"I have to pick some more ladies over the next few days for the show. You should come over to the studio and spend some time helping me decide who deserves a shot at romance."

"Me? Pick women for your show?" Lila smirks, but shakes her head. "No thanks, Brandon. My forte is to sell houses. Yours is to interview hundreds of women to decide which three are worth a shot at love with some hapless guy. They were totally screwing with his mind this afternoon, sweetheart. Where have you been finding them?"

I sigh. "Well, the list is getting shorter and shorter, I'm afraid. Some of the ladies don't show up when they are supposed to and we are forced to scramble to call in an alternate. It seems that the thousand dollars we offer now is not enough for some of the ladies we pre-screen. They walk away from that kind of money after counter offering ten times that amount."

"Surely they know better," Lila replies.

"Most don't," I tell her. "They're in Hollywood, after all. They want to be paid as if they are actresses on a sitcom. We simply can't do that." The problem has become more aggravating for me as well as for Lawson and some of the junior producers on the show over the last few months. In order to have a show that people will watch, we have to find attractive, younger women. Anyone over thirty-five is automatically tossed from the list. The ones who are left over know that they have value and try to leverage that fact to their advantage. Unfortunately, our sponsors are not willing to fork over ten grand for someone to answer questions and then go out on a date afterward. One thousand dollars should be enough, though it will soon not bring enough applications in to fill all of our shows completely.

"I hate the Hollywood scene," Lila says with a grimace on her face. "The whole lifestyle here is so over dramatic. If it weren't for our careers, I would want to move completely away from here."

I laugh. "It's *Hollywood,* honey." I lean forward and ask, "What if I were a guy on the show and you were one of the women? What would you have answered to some of those questions, Lila?" This is a question that I have asked my wife before, with mixed results. Sometimes she is playful enough to go along, but I cannot be sure that she wants to do so right now as she looks back at me.

"I don't know," she begins. "Some of the questions are loaded, Brandon. I suppose you and Lawson have something to do with that?" I nod my head. "Well, I guess if you asked me about what the first date should look like, I would want to go to a nice, quiet coffeehouse and enjoy some of their best coffee."

"Coffee," I reply with an audible grunt. "You would want to go get *coffee?*"

"That's why I normally don't want to answer these little scenarios you give me, Brandon. You always discount my answers."

"I don't discount them," I try to assure her. "I suppose I just think about it from the angle of a director and executive producer."

"But I'm your *wife,* Brandon."

"Not if you're on the show and I'm the guy," I tell her with a slight laugh. "Come on, give me a good answer. What would you want to do for a first date besides a coffeehouse. That's just too boring for the show, honey." I lean forward and put my elbows on the table as I wait for her to give me a better answer.

Lila sighs. "Well, I don't know. Maybe I would want to go to the beach and just take a long walk as the sun goes down. I really enjoy the feeling of the waves washing over my feet as the tide comes in."

"Now you're talking," I say with a grin. "And then what?"

"And then what?" Lila shakes her head. "I suppose you would want me to take you to a hotel and ride you hard, huh?" This time there is a sly expression that crosses my wife's face.

"That's probably a little more than you could say on camera."

"That one woman said that very thing this afternoon, Brandon."

"She said she likes to go up and down slowly and she didn't specifically say it was sex."

"Fuck, Brandon," Lila laughs loudly as she looks around the restaurant. Bringing her gaze back to me, she asks, "What did you think that she meant when she said it?"

"Oh, she meant it," I reply. "But she was careful about saying too much. She didn't say she would ride him cowgirl style while having sex."

My wife raises an eyebrow. "Do you guys coach them as to what they should say before the show?"

"A little," I admit. "Sometimes the women we get on the show are a little too eager to say whatever comes to mind. So, we have producers who run through the questions with them the morning before the show. It helps to reduce any problems that could pop up while the show is filming."

"Pop up," Lila says with a smile. "What if that happens?"

"What happens?"

"What if the guy gets hard during the show Brandon? Surely this has happened before."

"A few times," I reply. "We just get him a cold pack that he lays on his lap out of view of the camera. That normally takes care of that problem."

"Wow." My wife sits back in her chair and shakes her head. "That is brutal, my love. Just brutal."

"But effective." We laugh together as we each reach for our drinks. After we each take a sip, I ask, "What would you have thought of me if we had met on the show like the others do, Lila? Would you have wanted to go out with me?"

Her blue eyes scan my face before she gives me her answer. "Probably so, Brandon. You have to admit, though, that we met in a way that would not have been possible if you were running that show already."

"Yeah, you're right." Lila was studying at a university in Michigan when I traveled to Flint to see one of my great aunts. Had I been working in Hollywood at that time, I would have probably not strayed far from California. It is a good thing that we met like we did when we did.

"I would have chosen you, though," she replies. "You know I would have wanted only you, baby."

I reach across the table and take her hands into mine. "You would have made me really happy when you did, too."

"Happy enough to have needed a cold pack in your crotch, Brandon?" Lila smiles wickedly at me as I feel my face turn bright red.

"Probably so. Maybe I will show you tonight just how badly I would have needed that cold pack, my love."

"Oh, really?" Lila's eyes lock onto mine before I wave toward our server. It is time to get the ticket and pay so that I can take my wife home and capitalize on what is happening between us right now. Hot and horny, she is the sort of woman I can go all night long with in bed. I want Lila just now and I hope the heat between us remains through the drive home. Sex with her is unbelievable and I need to experience that tonight.

Chapter Three: Casting the Ladies

Lawson leans toward me as the sixteenth contestant applicant walks in through the conference room door. "I hope this one is a better one than the last," he tells me with a chuckle. We both feel the pressure to find the young women we need for next week's five days of shows.

"Good morning," I say with a smile to the woman as I look up and see her. "What is your name, please?"

"Sydney Cramer," she replies as she sits down in a chair at the long table.

"And you are twenty-eight?" I say as I look down at the clipboard on the table in front of me.

"Yes, I am," she replies. "I hope that's not too old," Sydney adds quickly.

"Oh, not at all," Lawson responds before I can answer. "We are fine up to about thirty-two or so. It really depends on the personality." There is a thick cloud of charm in the room as the host of the dating program works his magic with our young applicant. It is almost always this way, which is probably why he has bedded more than just a few of the women we have had on the show over the last three years.

"Are you single, Sydney?" I ask while looking up into her blue eyes.

A strained look appears on her face as she brushes a few strands of light brown hair from her forehead. "Um, yeah. That's why I'm here, right?"

I nod my head. "Well, I would hope so. Unfortunately, we have to ask before continuing with the interview." I allow a smile for the young woman as I recall an incident in the show last year. Another applicant selected for the show lied to us when she came in for her interview and it nearly cost us dearly in the publicity department. The young woman at that time told us she was single and unattached in any way, but we soon found out after the show had aired that she was, in fact, very married. Her husband saw the program and contacted us in a fit of rage, claiming that we had somehow conned her into doing the show even though she was married to him. When we confronted the contestant, she admitted that the only thing she wanted was the one thousand dollars we offered for her time. Though she was not selected by the young man for a date, things would have certainly gone downhill had such an event occurred and she only afterward confessed to her marital status. Keeping a lid on the whole thing would have been much more difficult had that happened.

"I don't have a boyfriend or anything like that," the woman seated in front of us replies. "At least, not for the last couple of months. I'm hoping this will give me a fresh start and maybe open up more possibilities."

"What sort of possibilities?" Lawson asks. He smiles at her, still working his charm as he eyes the young woman heavily.

Sydney shrugs her shoulders. "I've heard that some girls who get onto the show end up with offers for modeling or even some acting. I have always wanted to be an actor."

"An actor? Have you had any professional training as an actor?" I ask her as I jot down a few notes. During the interview process, we try to get as much information as we can for the questions that will be asked by the male participant on the show.

"No training," she replies. "Should I try to get some training?"

"That's not always necessary," Lawson tells her. "You look like you probably have a natural talent for it already." My cock gets a little hard as I look over and notice the way the show's host and the young woman are looking at each other. Lawson is an attractive man just shy of fifty years of age and most of the women on the show truly love being around him. Sydney appears to be no different as she smiles sheepishly at him.

"That's good. I don't want to waste any more time with college work or acting school. I have my Bachelor's degree, so I'm finished with that if I can help it."

"Bachelor's degree in what field?" I ask.

She smiles. "Business data management. I have been working the last three years for a company in San Bernardino."

"Very nice." I nod my head as I write down this information as well.

"Height and weight?" Lawson asks.

Seemingly offended, Sydney replies. "Well, um, I'm five-six and weigh about one-forty." The young woman swallows hard as I look at her. She is probably lying just a little on the weight, but she is attractive nonetheless. The applicant is certainly within our guidelines and very well groomed, so I have a good feeling that we will be asking her to appear on the show soon.

"Very nice," Lawson says with a smile. "And what sort of date do you hope to have if you are selected by a young man?"

Shrugging her shoulders, Sydney replies, "I don't know. I guess it would be nice if it were something cozy and romantic. Maybe a walk on a pier somewhere on the coast or a drive up the highway into the hills. I'm up for just about anything if I'm chosen to be a date." She smiles widely, her beautiful white teeth showing just a little between her full red lips.

"Sydney, thank you for your time," I say as I nod my head at her. "We have your contact information and we will be in contact if we decide to ask you to be on the show."

She smiles. "Thank you for seeing me today." Sydney stands to her feet and straightens her blouse before turning to walk out of the conference room. An assistant closes the door behind her before I turn to look at Lawson. "You've flirted with every one of them so far today," I observe. "Are you being as objective as you should be?"

"Of course I am," the host replies. "You know me, Brandon. I can't help but have a little fun with them when they come in here."

"Yes, but they aren't for *you*, Lawson. Let's keep things professional, alright?"

"Name one thing I have said or done today that was not professional," he retorts with a sly grin.

"Oh, come on," I laugh. "You know that you were flirting with Sydney a moment ago. We have to be careful that we don't put off the wrong image for the show."

"I put off the right image for the show," Lawson argues. "The audience expects me to flirt a little, Brandon. You know that. We've talked about it several times before."

"Yeah, I get that, but taking the ladies out when they don't make the cut isn't the sort of thing that we need on the front page of a tabloid."

"Who really cares, though?" he asks. "I'm a single man who can enjoy my time with a lovely woman just like any other guy. Don't worry, Brandon, I never go out with any of the ladies that are chosen for the show or rejected later."

I shake my head. "You are going to regret doing that one day. We have had a few mentally unstable ones in the past that you have had sex with, Lawson. If you knock one of them up..."

"I'm fixed," he interrupts. "Besides, we have been weeding them out pretty well recently, haven't we? None of them have gone over the deep end in the last year or so."

"No, not yet, but..."

"As long as we stick to the approved applicant list we will be just fine. The background checks have helped too, right?" Lawson focuses his dark eyes on me and I think about how much time has been devoted to looking into the female applicants' lives. We have a small team of producers who spend almost all of their time looking into social media accounts, applications, and even state police background checks before we even speak with any of the women who have applied. Though the standards in place do seem to be helpful, there is still no guarantee that things will always work out the way they are expected to. There are just too many variables still out there after we have finished our work looking into the women on our list.

"Just be careful," I say quietly as I look up and nod my head toward the assistant at the door to the large conference room. She opens the door and allows the next applicant to walk in. Smiling, I motion toward a chair and say to her, "Have a seat."

"Thank you." The young redhead smiles as she looks from me to Lawson and then back again. "Tracy Young, Venice, California."

"Oh, good. That clears out a couple of questions." Lawson smiles at her before looking down and making notes on his pad.

"So, Tracy, I want to thank you for coming in today." I feel my cock flex a little as I think about how beautiful the young woman happens to be. We are constantly on the lookout for women just like her. "How old are you?"

"Twenty-two," she answers. "I'm a senior at Cal State this year." Tracy's green eyes lock onto mine as she offers another soft smile. "Are you married?"

"What?" I look from her to Lawson, who immediately smirks in my direction. Turning my attention back to her, I answer, "That's really not something I generally get asked."

"I'm sorry," she replies. "It's just that you look like a nice guy and I was wondering if there is a lucky woman in your life." Tracy moves her hand toward the side of her face and then pushes some hair over her ear. "Please forgive me if I offended you."

"Oh, no, I'm not offended," I reply quickly. "You just took me by surprise, that's all. The answer to your question is that yes, I am married."

"Ah." Tracy appears disappointed as she continues to look into my eyes. "I'm glad to hear you have found someone."

"Alright then," Lawson says with a chuckle as he pulls me out of the trance that I have suddenly found myself in. "So, you are looking for a man to call your own, Tracy?"

"Yeah, I'm looking for someone," she answers while turning and looking at the show's host for a moment. It does not take long for her to turn her eyes back to me. "But I really just wanted to meet you guys. I'm a huge fan of the show and it would be a huge honor to be on it."

"Thank you," I manage to reply. Though I can practically feel Lawson's stare from my right, I refuse to turn and look at him. "So, what sort of date would you like to have if the man on the show selects you,

Tracy?" I sit quietly as my johnson becomes completely stiff. I want her so badly right now that I am having trouble just concentrating on the questions I have written down on the clipboard in front of me.

"What would *you* like if you were on a date with someone?" she asks. "If you were the guy and you picked me, what would we do?" Tracy smiles sheepishly as she folds her hands into her lap.

"Um, well…" I find myself at a loss for words as I feel my body shake.

"He loves getting close and very intimate," Lawson offers. "What would you want to do with my friend here if he wanted to go out with you?"

Tracy blushes a little but then says as she looks at me, "You can have me, if you want. I mean, if that's what it takes to be on the show."

"What?"

Tracy opens the top of her dress a little to expose her small, soft breasts and the small pink nipples on them. "I can give you a blow job right now if you like."

"Holy fuck…"

"I think we've seen enough," Lawson says as my jaw drops.

"Did I say something I shouldn't have?" the young woman asks as she closes the front of her dress and stands to her feet.

"No, I think we have what we need to make a decision. We will be calling you as soon as we have a spot open up, alright?" He walks over to her and escorts Tracy to the door before letting her out. The producer there follows her out and Lawson closes the door behind them. "Damn, you can really pick them, huh?"

"Pick them? I met her when you did just a few minutes ago."

"I mean when you flirt, Brandon. She's hot and she's willing. Tracy was ready for a little freakiness to prove her worth to be on the show." He laughs quietly as he walks to the other end of the room and opens up a small refrigerator. The show's host pulls out two small bottles of liquor and walks back to his seat. After handing me one, he asks, "Would you have done her if I had not been here?"

"Are you serious?" I chuckle. "I don't do that, Lawson. That's in *your* territory."

"Sure, it normally is, but I could see it all over you, buddy. You wanted her badly."

I grit my teeth as I open the small bottle of whiskey. "Fuck this day," I growl lightly before taking a drink of the strong liquid.

"Look, if you would prefer to do the rest of these without me, I could...

"Oh, for crying out loud." We both have a good laugh together and straighten up our notes before moving on to the next applicant. Though I refute Lawson's claim, I would have likely allowed things to have moved a bit further along had he not been in the room with me. I too have sexual urges and I am often attracted to the women we interview. The difference between us, though, is that I have managed to keep those urges in check over the last few years. Thankfully that record remains unblemished as we await the next woman on our list.

Chapter Four: An Unfortunate Turn

"Where the hell is she?" I mumble as I look hard at one of the junior show producers. "Angela is supposed to be here."

"I called her and she said that she is stuck in traffic. She's trying." The young producer, a man in his late twenties, is rattled by the way I have come at him about the absence of not just one of the women selected to be on the show, but also the alternate who was supposed to be on standby at the studio in the event she needed to fill in for someone.

"I can't run this fucking show without three women," I growl as I look over at Lawson. A part of me is irritated that he seems altogether too calm about the whole situation. "This is going to go right into the toilet in an hour if we don't do something."

"Hey, I'm just the show's host, right?" He laughs as he walks up to me. "Have you tried calling some of the women on the list from last week's interviews?"

I sigh. "I tried calling several of them and was told that they were either not able to make it here in time or that they were no longer interested." Shaking my head, I tell Lawson, "It is getting harder and harder to find anyone who is serious about doing the show."

"Maybe for the ladies, but we have more than a hundred guys raring to go."

"We can't put a guy up there in one of the women's spots," I reply. "Sean isn't gay."

"It would be a real hoot, though, right?" He chuckles and pats me on the arm before suggesting, "Try to find one of your friends or something. Tell her that you only need her for a short time and that we can change the questions up so that Sean doesn't select her. That would work, right?"

"I don't know, Lawson. What a guy does can be so unpredictable."

"We can tell him that the third one is a dud, alright? I'm sure he'll play along, Brandon. He seems like the sort of guy who is easygoing enough."

"No," I spit back immediately. "We can't do that. It would fuck up the whole dynamic if he was aware of a fake. The audience, both here and at home, would know that something was up early into the show."

"Then find someone." Lawson levels his eyes at me before turning to walk away. He is right; I have to find a replacement fast.

I think for a while about the friends that I have who I could call on a moment's notice. Though there are a few, some of them are often busy during the day and so there would be no guarantee that any of them could show up this afternoon. Others are either married or not really interested in what we do here in the studio. One of my wife's friends once told me that she would rather be buried alive than to ever appear on a dating show on television. As I consider this, an idea suddenly comes to mind. "Fuck. It's right there." I pull my cell phone from my pocket and begin to dial a number.

The phone rings a few times before I hear a voice on the other end of the line. "Hello?"

"Hey, Lila!" I say with some enthusiasm as I greet my wife. "How are things at work today?"

"Well, I suppose they're going great, Brandon. How are things with you?"

I nervously smile to myself as I watch the crew onstage making the final adjustments for the show. "Okay, I guess. There is a problem that has come up here, though. Could you come to the studio and help me with something for the rest of the afternoon, honey?" My heart races as I ask for my wife's help.

"Help you with what? Sweetheart, I have clients coming at four to see a house."

"You'll be finished long before then," I promise. "I just need your help with something during the show this afternoon. Could you come?" My heart races as I await her response. Though I have asked Lila in the past to come by and help me with things such as selecting female applicants for an interview, I have never considered asking her to stand in for one of them.

"Brandon, is it that important?" I get the sense that Lila really does not want to come to the studio, but I know that she will if I persist.

"It's very important," I confirm. "Can you get here quickly, though? The show starts in about an hour and I need your help before then."

Lila sighs, but replies, "I'll be there in twenty, Brandon. I can't stay for long, though. This client is too important."

"No problem. I'll get you out of here in no time," I promise her as I feel goosebumps forming on my neck and arms. "I love you, honey."

"I love you too, baby," she answers before we hang up the phone. I put away my cell phone and look over at where Lawson is standing. He gives me a questioning look and I respond with a thumbs-up. After nodding his head, the host turns around and continues to work on his notes at the podium where he will guide everything during the show.

"Should you tell him?" I ask myself as I consider the person coming to take the missing woman's spot today. "No, keep it quiet," I answer quickly. Though Lawson and I have worked together for three years, he has not met my wife yet. Studio parties are just not her thing, so I have not insisted that she attend. She is unknown to my coworkers, which is a positive thing as of right now. Walking back to one side of the stage, I sit down and look through a file folder with the other two women's information. As I begin to write down Lila's stats, I take a deep breath and focus on my work while awaiting her arrival. It is not long before she gets here, though, after I become fully engaged in my work on the clipboard. Soon, a producer comes to my side.

"Brandon, there is a woman here who says that you asked for her?" I look up and see my wife.

"Yeah, send her over," I tell him. He turns and waves Lila over to me and then leaves as I begin to speak to her. "Thank you so much for this, honey."

She smiles while looking at me with her blue eyes. "Anything for my husband. What do you need?"

I look to my right and wave at one of our makeup stylists. She comes over and I say to her, "Summer, this is Lila. Could you take her back and get her dressed and made up for the show?"

"Wait, *what?*" My wife is confused as she looks hard at me.

"Do me this favor," I reply. "I don't have anyone else and this is really important. Don't worry, okay?" She suddenly realizes what I want from her, but instead of asking more questions she goes with Summer to get ready. Just fifteen minutes later, Lawson and I are in our positions and ready to start the show. He receives the questions meant for the third woman, my wife, and nods his head. The interesting thing is that Lawson has never met Lila before. It should be interesting to see whether he realizes she is my wife.

The show starts off smoothly, with the young man, Sean, interacting with each woman as if there has been no change. The questions I have written seem to be leading him away from choosing Lila for a date, which was the intent behind them. Unfortunately, I realize that Lawson has decided to go a little off-script after Sean calls on woman number three, my wife.

"Let's jazz things up," Lawson says with a wild grin on his face. "Lila, Sean has talked about having a nice date for dinner and then possibly a walk along the beach. You have said that you are not the sentimental type, so let me ask you something. If Sean were to instead take you straight to a hotel for your date, what would you say and do?" My heart races as I reach down and try to buzz Lawson's earpiece to let him know that I want to talk to him. However, he has decided to turn off the little piece of equipment so that he can focus on what is happening on the stage. We have talked about this habit before, but apparently the show's host has not learned from earlier admonishments concerning such.

"Straight to a hotel?" Lila's eyes look toward the side of one of the cameras from where I am watching this all unfold. "What do you mean by that?"

"Well, I think Sean is a young man who would love to have a reason to consider you, Lila. So far, you haven't been very interested in anything he has said. The question, then, would be whether you would prefer a quick and hot time in bed as opposed to getting to know each other over a meal." Some in the studio audience gasp, but the engineers in the control room have likely made certain that the sounds are muffled in the program broadcast.

"I don't know..."

"I think you sound hot," Sean tells my wife as he squirms around in his chair. "But, you sound really stuffy, too. Is that what you would prefer, Lila? Do you want to go straight to a hotel or is there something else that would make you happy?"

"Happy?" She shakes her head as she looks at the studio audience. My wife understands that I need her to put on a good show for me, so she gathers her thoughts before answering, "I like a lot of things. A nice dinner would be fun, but I don't know you very well. So, you would have to take things slowly with me." Lila bites her bottom lip as she again looks at where I am standing nearby. My cock stiffens as I look back into her eyes.

"I can take things slowly, Lila. Don't you worry." I do not like the sound of Sean's response as he smiles. Suddenly, it appears that his choice for a woman is changing. I was certain moments ago he would choose the first woman, Monica, but there is an attraction for my wife that lies in his mannerisms.

"Dammit," I mutter as I shake my head and cross my arms.

"What's wrong?" one of the camera operators says quietly to me as I stare at the stage.

"Nothing," I reply with a sigh. "It's just that nothing is working out the way I had expected." I continue to stand and watch the show unfold before me as I think of the hell I will pay once Lila and I get back home. I called her to the studio under the pretense of needing her help, which I did, but this was nowhere near what she expected when she drove over here. Whatever choice Sean makes, I am going to be sleeping on the couch tonight, if not worse. I have royally fucked up, and Lila will be certain to remind me of that later.

Chapter Five: A Great Guy

My wife is not happy at all as we walk into the front door of our house together. Her face is still very pink after she stood on the stage with Sean in the studio and now we both worry how the date can possibly go on after I asked her to stand in for the missing woman and her alternate this afternoon.

"It's bad enough that people I know will see it, Brandon," Lila complains as she walks straight to the kitchen with me a step or two behind her. "What the fuck were you thinking?" Her blue eyes turn to me for just a moment before she opens the refrigerator door and pulls out a bottle of wine cooler. After opening the top, Lila takes a quick sip and then sits back against the countertop. "I can't believe you put me in that position."

"Look, I can fix this," I tell her. "I can tell Sean that the date has to happen at a restaurant and then it's all over. I'm sure he'll understand."

Lila shakes her head. "This isn't happening, Brandon. You need to call that guy and tell him there has been some mistake. I won't do this." My wife turns and faces the kitchen sink while looking out through the window toward our backyard. I realize that I have really screwed everything up by having her come to the studio and standing in for one of the women who should have been there. Though I cannot do anything to change what happened earlier on live television, I need to convince her that she has to go through with some sort of date to keep any rumors from spreading about the show.

"Please, honey," I begin as I reach out and put a hand on her shoulder. My wife's petite body trembles slightly as I trace the contour of her shoulders with my fingers. "I can't afford any of this to get out to the public. If Sean begins to suspect that you were a stand-in and not the real thing, he might go to the studio execs and complain. Hell, he might even go to the press, Lila. Just go out with him for dinner and that will be all there is to it. I promise." My mind races as I think about the oddity of setting up my own wife for a date with another man. Even so, there really is no harm in Lila having dinner with the young man. Rarely does any one of our dating couples go any further than dinner and light conversation anyway.

"Brandon." My wife shakes her head and gives me a strained look before taking another drink of her wine cooler. She then walks to the living room and has a seat on the leather couch. Sitting back in the fat cushions, Lila pulls up her feet and tries to relax with the small bottle in her hand. "Why didn't you find another woman? You have interviews with them all the time, right? You could have called any one of them to fill in."

I shake my head. "No, I tried. There was just no more time, honey. We needed you there and I'm sorry about being so mysterious about it at first when I called you. I should have told you upfront what I had planned, but then I was afraid..." My voice trails off as I sit down beside my wife.

"You were afraid that I would say no." Lila grimaces as she finishes what I was trying to say. "That's pretty fucked up, sweetheart."

"Yeah, it's fucked up," I admit. "Lots of things about my business are fucked up, and sometimes we have to deal with it. I needed you and you came to my rescue. Thank you for that." I realize that the appreciation I am trying to show seems shallow and practically worthless at this point to my wife, but I truly am grateful for her. Though I have put her into a challenging position, I know she can cope with what she needs to do with Sean. After all, the dinner thing is purely platonic, at least for her part.

"What's he like?" she asks me. "I mean, what does he do for work? I didn't quite catch that during the show."

I nod my head. "His name is Sean Richards and he is an investment advisor with a local firm."

"An investment advisor? He's pretty young for that, right?"

"Well, he's twenty-five," I reply. "When we performed the background check we found that he has become a great advisor with his firm. The guy is rock solid and has no criminal history."

"Oh, that's comforting," Lila replies snarkily. "At least I won't have to worry about being robbed by the guy." I cannot help but smile a little as I observe the expression on my wife's face. "Stop it," she says after a moment of my staring at her.

"What?"

"Stop looking at me like that. You do that when you get horny and I'm not in the mood for anything like that, Brandon."

I realize suddenly that I have a hardon in my pants. "Oh, this?" I reach down and tug around the fabric where I am pitching a tent. "Do you want it, baby?"

"Brandon, don't." My wife laughs a little as she shakes her head. "We're talking about the guy from the studio, remember? You shouldn't be getting horny over that sort of thing."

Reaching over, I put an arm around her shoulders. "Would you like to suck it?"

"What?" Lila laughs as she pushes my arm away. "You're like a teenage boy looking for his first blow job. Stop it."

I reach down and unzip my pants. It has been at least a week since the last time my wife and I have been intimate with each other and I have noticed the absence of affection every night as we have slept in bed together. There are times when Lila will become less interested in sex while my own drive continues to be heightened. Oh, how I wish that she would just give me a nice blow job right now.

"Brandon, what are you doing? Are you serious?" Lila's eyes grow wide as I tug on my cock with my hand.

"Just do this for me, honey. I'm a nice guy just like Sean. Suck me and pretend that it's him."

"You're out of your mind," she giggles before reaching toward my manhood with her small, soft hand. I pull back my own hand as my wife begins to slowly move her fingers over the end of my hard shaft.

"Oh, shit, baby," I moan as I pre-come into her fingers. Lila takes the natural lubricant and spreads it all over the tip of my johnson as my hips grind into the couch cushion beneath me.

"Do you like this, Sean?" my wife asks as she uses the other man's name. This causes me to stiffen even more as I think about the young man with Lila. Why am I thinking such a thing? Do I *really* want her to be sexual with him in any way when they go on their date?

"Fuck, honey. Oh, shit, you are driving me crazy." She pulls hard on my cock and I pre-come even more. Then, after smiling wickedly at me, Lila goes down and takes my manhood into her soft mouth. "Baby," I moan as I feel the end of my long pole reach the back of her throat. My wife is an incredible giver of blow jobs and I have always enjoyed any oral treatment from her. Having gone a while without any relief, this is a nice surprise.

Lila pulls up slowly with her mouth as her lips hug the sides of my cock tightly. I buck a little in my seat as she does this over and over again. "Honey," I say as I lay my head back and enjoy the sensation of her tongue on the underside of my phallus. Her small hand moves into my pants and finds my balls. Lila gently massages them as she continues to work on siphoning my sex organ.

"Holy shit," I groan as my toes point. "Fuck, I'm going to come, Lila. Swallow it, okay? Swallow it as if you are swallowing Sean's spunk. I hope you suck him off. Fuck, you need to suck him. *Ohhhhh...*" I come hard into my wife's mouth as she pushes the end of my cock to the back of her mouth. *"Ahhhh...ohhhh...ohhhh..."* Putting my hands on the back of her head, I release my wad into her throat and enjoy the feeling of Lila swallowing each spurt for me. *"Ohhhh...fuck...FUCK!!!"* After several more spurts into her mouth, I feel my orgasm begin to pass and I lay my head back once again. My wife finishes swallowing all of my warm man gravy before she pulls back from me and reaches for her wine cooler on the table at the end of the couch.

After taking a drink, she asks, "Did you like pretending that you were Sean?"

I turn my head and look at her. "I'm sorry about that, honey. I know you don't like that sort of thing, but I couldn't help myself." Lila is rarely in the mood to pretend that we are other people during sex. As a matter of fact, she is fairly utilitarian about the whole act of sex when it comes to the bedroom. Fantasies are sometimes discussed, but rarely undertaken as a part of our lovemaking.

"It's okay," she replies with a small smile. "I know you like the idea of me being with other men, Brandon. We've talked about that a little before. I think that is probably the real reason you called me to be on the show."

Shaking my head, I tell her, "I didn't think about that at all when I called you, Lila. I swear I didn't."

My wife nods her head. "Yeah, okay. Still, you have some kind of fantasy going on inside your head now, don't you? I know you too well, Brandon. You can't hide that sort of thing from me so easily."

I press my lips together and nod my head. "Maybe I do have some kind of vulgar thought process when it comes to you, my love, but I don't mean anything by it. I don't expect you to have sex with Sean. All I need you to do is have dinner with him so that no one will be any the wiser about the whole screwy episode today. Trust me, you will be able to call things off after dinner." I offer a smile to my wife and hope that she is willing to go along. To my relief, she nods her head and smiles back at me.

"Fine, I'll have dinner with him. However, I will not be giving the guy head, Brandon. Nothing sexual is going to happen between me and that man. Do I have your word on this?"

"Yes, of course," I answer. "Nothing at all sexual, honey. You can end it whenever you like after we get a few video shots for the show. All will be well after the fact, right?"

"Right." Though Lila appears to be apprehensive of the whole thing, she seems ready to help me keep the show in the best light possible with our audience and the studio executives. That is all I can ask of my wife now that I have already taken advantage of her willingness to help me. I am so thankful to have someone like her in my life who is willing to step in and be supportive of me the way she has recently and in the past. One day I will have to figure out a way to repay her for her kindness. Hopefully this repayment will be sooner rather than later.

Chapter Six: A Romantic Dinner

41

The studio executives have given us a list of restaurants that we are allowed to take the new couple to with the expenses covered by the studio. This means that most of the restaurants we visit are somewhat nicer than what some young couples would typically visit on a first date. The restaurant my wife and Sean are visiting today is inside an exclusive hotel, which makes this a bit weird for me as we set up for the weekend afternoon shoot.

"Set up over there," I say to the cameraman as I look around the small room the studio has rented from the hotel's restaurant. "You can get them both in the booth together." The Italian eatery is more than seventy years old and filled with pictures of past actors and other famous people who have stopped by over that period of time. Lila and I have eaten here before, which makes setting up here even more odd to me as I think about whether any of the wait staff will recognize us. This is normally not a problem for me, but since my wife is standing in for another woman, it would be embarrassing to be called out by someone who works here.

"You guys are with the show," a server says as she works to help set out the silverware and napkins for the couple. "I'm Tammy." She offers her hand and I take it to shake. Lawson has opted to not be here tonight, which of course is on par for the way we do things. In many instances I am not involved in the filming during the dates either, but for obvious reasons this one holds a particular interest for me.

"We are," I reply as the server pulls her hand back. "I'm Brandon."

"Yeah, I've seen you on the show a few times," she replies. "Where's Lawson?"

"Lawson." I smile as I realize the young woman is not as smitten with the sight of me as she is with the thought that she might actually get to meet the host of the show. "Well, he isn't going to be here this afternoon. I'm sorry if that's disappointing."

Tammy smiles. "It's okay. I thought I would ask anyway." She turns and motions toward the table. "Is this what you wanted?"

"Yeah, that looks great," I reply. "Is the meal almost ready?"

"It's ready whenever you are," she answers. "The chef is holding it in the warmer until you have them seated and ready."

I turn and nod my head toward one of the producers. He then walks out through the door of the small meeting room and I look back at the server. "When we begin to film, you can come up and pour the wine, alright? Then you will need to leave."

"So, I don't come back at all?"

"Not unless we cut filming and then call for you to come back. If you wouldn't mind waiting at the other end of the room, that would be great."

"I'll be on TV, then?"

"For about five or ten seconds," I promise. "At least long enough for your parents or someone else to get to see you on the screen. Remember, this is all taped and will air at the end of the month in our two-hour special with the other dates." It is the one thing that servers and other restaurant staff always love to hear whenever they are a part of the production of a meal date. Getting on television is at the very least a prideful moment to share with their family and friends. On rare occasions, there could even be a casting director watching who will end up calling to put someone into a commercial or even as an extra in a television show. Though I do not fancy myself a career maker in the slightest, I do have to admit that there have been a number of people who have benefited from appearing briefly on the show.

"I'll be back there, then." Tammy smiles widely at me before turning and walking toward a small table in the back of the private dining room. There are two other servers and a manager already sitting there so that they may be of service immediately if we need anything.

"Here they come," The cameraman says as he turns on his camera and points it toward the couple coming through the door. My heart races as I see Lila followed by Sean enter the room. She is so sexy in her simple blue cocktail dress.

"Just continue to walk toward the table," the producer off to the side says as they make their way inside. "Remember, Lila will sit first, and then Sean." The sound of the producer's voice will be cut in the final edit of the video and some background narrative added. These things have become very standard for everyone involved after so many episodes of the show.

My wife has a seat on one side of the booth and Sean joins her as he sits down on the other side. The cameraman follows them both and instructions are called out to them from the side by a producer. Wine is soon brought in by Tammy and she pours each their drink. They have a sip and Lila smiles at the young man in front of her. Her eyes never turn to look for me or to question what is going on. As a matter of fact, she appears to be having a very nice time with the young man.

"Nice," one of the producers whispers into my ear. I turn to see the young woman standing just to my side. "They seem to be hitting it off, right?"

I shrug my shoulders. "I suppose they are. She's about eight years older than him, though."

"Really?" The producer seems to be surprised by this bit of information. "I would have guessed her to be about his age. Lila has done a great job keeping herself looking so young." The young woman smiles and turns to confer with another producer nearby. My eyes move back to where the couple is sitting and I consider the fact that I have only brought my wife to the studio once or twice over the last three years. Lawson has never met her and I have only once or twice mentioned her name to him, which is why I got away with putting Lila into the role that needed to be filled at the last moment. Right now I feel decidedly embarrassed for my decision to keep her hidden away from the others at the studio. After all, she is my better half.

"You are beautiful," I hear Sean say, likely at the direction of a producer nearby. "Are you enjoying your time here, Lila?"

She nods her head. "It's a beautiful restaurant." Lila takes a sip of wine and then the main course is brought into place before them. At this point, the camera is shut off part of the time as the couple have some rare moments of privacy together.

"We are going to follow them, right?" Craig, the cameraman, asks as he walks over to me.

"Follow them where?" I ask with surprise.

"You know, like we often do. If they like each other enough they might head upstairs, right?"

"Uh, no," I say without thinking first. "I mean, I don't see where they are making that much of a connection."

Craig looks at them and then back at me while chuckling. "Oh, I don't know. They seem pretty interested in each other." He turns and walks over to another table where the restaurant staff has provided the crew some water. As the cameraman gets a drink, I turn my attention back to where Lila and Sean are sitting. They are both deeply involved in conversation as they enjoy the meal in front of them. This is absolutely not the outcome I had expected when I spoke to my wife just this morning. We had agreed that at some point she would tell the young man that she was just not feeling things were going well and would excuse herself. It has happened so many times before. Unfortunately, Lila appears to have forgotten the plan. I walk closer to the couple and listen to what they are saying.

"And you are probably very talented as well," I hear Sean say to Lila.

"Maybe I am, but I've never tried rock climbing without equipment. That must be really scary."

"Exhilarating," he replies. "There's just nothing like it in the world. Not even sex." The comment causes my johnson to stiffen a little as I pretend to be looking at some of the pictures on the wall nearby.

"Not even sex? Really?" Lila laughs. "That's a bit extreme, don't you think? Sex has got to be the best thing when it comes to adventure."

Sean shakes his head. "Not from what I have experienced. The women I have been with were not exactly the sort of people to tell my family about."

"So, no serious relationships?"

"Not since about sixth grade," Sean tells my wife, causing them both to laugh. "You are by far the most intelligent of any woman I have had dinner with in the last couple of years." The young man reaches over and takes Lila's hand, causing a small streak of jealousy to rise inside me. Sure, I am turned on by what is happening between them, but there is some limitation to that as I worry that something could develop between them.

"And, action," I hear a producer say as the camera once again comes up and begins to take in what the couple are doing at the table. I back away and watch as they take subtle cues from those around them as they finish their meal and have another glass of wine. After another half-hour or so, Sean gets up and helps Lila to her feet. They then turn and walk out of the small room. Craig follows with the camera and I go just behind him as the camera continues to run.

"What are they doing?" I say under my breath as they walk up to the front desk of the exclusive hotel. "They should be going outside."

"The execs told us to cover a room if they wanted one," the same young producer from earlier says as she walks up to me. "It's a new thing now."

"What?" I turn and look hard at the young woman before looking back at Sean and Lila. Without looking in my direction, my wife walks toward the elevator with the young man and our cameraman captures the moment with his camera. I walk up to the hotel desk and address the clerk. "Which room did you give them?"

The man looks up at me and then at the producers behind me. "Um, the one you guys paid for."

"Which one specifically?" I ask.

"Six-nineteen," he replies. "Like I said, you guys paid for it and they have it until tomorrow morning at ten o'clock." I turn and walk toward the elevator and Craig follows me with the camera.

"What are you doing?" he asks quietly as the others stand in the lobby while watching what is going on.

"I'm going upstairs to stop this," I answer.

"Stop it? We never stop couples from doing whatever they want after a date, Brandon. You know that."

"This time is different," I tell him. My mind races as I try to come up with an answer to the question that I know is going to be coming from Craig next.

"How is it different?" I press the elevator button and wait for the door to open without answering him. Then, I step inside and he continues to follow me. "This is weird, man."

"It's not as weird as you might think," I say as the doors close and we begin the trip up to the room on the sixth floor. It is not long before we are in front of the hotel room door.

"The execs will be pissed if you bother them," he tells me as he sets his camera down on the floor nearby. "You know how they can be. We were told to only film to the elevator and to allow them to have their privacy after that. Sometimes they have sex and sometimes they don't."

"Wait, are you saying this has already been going on? I've been on some of the dates with you, Craig, and I have never seen the studio pay for this sort of thing."

"Oh, the paying thing is new, but the elevator shots are not so new. You have just never stuck around to see that part." He looks me over and asks, "Do you have a thing for this girl, Brandon?"

My face turns red as I shake my head. "Of course not. It's just that after interviewing both of them, I know they are absolutely wrong for each other. I don't want them to do something that they might regret later. You can understand that, right?"

"You can't bother them, man," Craig replies. "You know that the bosses will have your head. They might fire me too." There is a measure of fear in his voice as he stands beside me in the hallway. It is just now that we both hear something through the door.

"Wait, what's that?" I put my ear to the door and listen for a moment. Feeling my face changing color, I soon pull away from the door. Craig then does the same.

"Holy shit," he says to me with a smile on his face. "They're banging in there, Brandon."

"No shit," I growl as I sit down on the floor beside the door.

"No, man, I mean they are *really* banging in there. She's practically shrieking. Holy hell, I think she's already getting off with the guy."

My body shakes as I think about what I can do at this point. Lila is having sex with Sean just out of my view. Though I was completely turned on by the idea of Sean fucking her, I never thought that it would actually happen. The feeling of jealousy I had just a while ago in the restaurant now seems insignificant compared to the feelings I am having now.

The sounds coming out of the room go on for some time before they finally end. Craig allows a smile on his face as he picks up the camera. "I think they're finished. We should go, Brandon. The bosses will want to hear about this."

I look up at him before standing to my feet. "We don't need to tell them about this, Craig. Like you said earlier, they really don't want us bothering the couples. They might think we were too much involved with what they have done in that room."

"This is a huge deal. They really went at it inside there, right? We could weave in some sort of additional storyline here. The execs will love it, man. We have to tell them." Craig turns and moves quickly toward the elevators. I begin to do the same until I feel compelled to stop and look at the door again. Lila is most likely lying with Sean while naked in the same bed. She fucked another man and I witnessed it, though not visually. How will this affect our marriage? I can only guess at what she might say to me later. Turning, I leave the hallway and ride the elevator back to the lobby below.

Chapter Seven: Surprisingly Fun

49

The evening is late as I sit on the back terrace of our suburban home looking over Los Angeles in the distance. Lila and I decided a couple of years ago to move out of the city to try to find some solitude for our private time together. Often on a Saturday evening we have a drink of wine on the terrace together, but tonight I find myself swallowing gulps of port wine as I run the events of today through my mind.

"Hello," I hear a voice say behind me. I turn to see Lila standing just outside the terrace doors. "Do you have another glass?" I nod my head toward a glass next to the chilled bottle of wine. It was not as if I had brought it out here for my wife's benefit when she finally returned, but an old habit from the many times before that we have spent time out here together. If I had thought much about it, I would have probably left the glass in the kitchen out of spite.

"Where's Sean?" I ask as I sit back in my chair and stare at the lights in the valley.

Lila sits down in a chair nearby. "He went home. Did you think that I would bring him here?"

I shrug my shoulders. "I wasn't sure what you might do. You could have brought him over and maybe took him to bed with you again." It is a shot at my wife that I cannot keep myself from taking as I simmer over what happened this afternoon at the hotel. Though it is not like me to pout over our disagreements, I feel as if I am somewhat entitled at this point.

"What do you mean by that?" she asks quietly.

"You know what I mean," I retort. Looking over at her, I add, "You went to a room with him, Lila. Did you really think I wouldn't see the two of you go up there?"

She smiles nervously. "Honestly, Brandon, nothing happened. All we did was go up there and talk for a while. He really is a nice guy, just as you told me that he was."

Shaking my head, I reply, "We *heard* you, Lila. Craig the cameraman and I both heard what was going on inside that fucking room. You can't sit there and lie to me about this. You fucked Sean."

The color in my wife's face suddenly leaves as she sits and stares at me. A part of me is glad to see the sudden reaction from her, but then another part feels badly for her. Never before have I confronted Lila about anything concerning another man, especially when it comes to sex. Even though I want to go to her and apologize for the way I am behaving, I sit still and simply stare back at her. She deserves to feel uncomfortable, right? I am not the one who has had sex with another person, *she* is. This is all on Lila now and I have no reason to feel sorry for her.

Lila swallows slowly before telling me, "You were mistaken, sweetie. We didn't have sex. You must have heard the television or maybe even some sound from another room. Sean was a perfect gentleman the entire time, I promise." She focuses her blue eyes on me as she waits to see whether her explanation passes whatever analysis I put it to.

"No," I reply after a moment of consideration. "I can see it in your face, Lila. You screwed the guy. Why are you lying to me even though Craig and I caught you in the act?"

"You don't know what you are talking about." My wife stands to her feet and puts down the empty wine glass she has been holding the last few minutes. She turns and walks into the house and I get up to follow her inside.

"I know about what you did," I call out as I follow her toward the master bedroom. "I asked you to help with him, but I didn't ask you to *fuck* him, Lila. You didn't have to fuck him."

She stops in the doorway of our bedroom. "Why did you put me in that show again, Brandon? Was it something about none of the other women not being able to come and fill in? Bullshit. I call bullshit on that story, Brandon. You're a stupid fuck if you think that I believed that for one second." My wife then turns and walks toward the bathroom while pulling off her blue dress.

"Dammit, Lila, you know that I needed you for the show to keep things on balance. I have the studio execs constantly breathing down my neck. One slip-up and the program could be canceled. I'm making bank off this damn thing, honey, and I don't want to lose it just yet. Another three or four years and I should be able to trade off my experience there for a better gig."

"To do what?" she barks back at me as she pulls off her bra. "To direct or produce another daytime show? No one likes that fucking show anyway, Brandon. I don't personally know of a single person who watches it."

"Six million people watch it across the country every day," I reply. "That may sound like small potatoes to you, but that is a huge audience for that sort of show. The studio is making a lot of money off it, so I make a nice paycheck as well. As long as things run smoothly, I keep getting that paycheck."

"And I have to stand in for one of your little whores," she retorts as she drops her thong panties to the floor. Turning, Lila reaches down to turn on the faucet for the bathtub. She enjoys bathing more than showering, so our master bedroom's bathroom has both amenities.

"What the hell is that?" I say as I walk up to her and run my finger along her valley. Lila starts to stand up, but I push her back down so that her hands are on the edge of the tub. "Dried cum. Did you even ask him to wear a fucking condom?"

Lila's eyes grow wide as she looks back at me. "Brandon, it's not cum." I run my hands over her soft, round ass as I look at where Sean has left his mark on my wife. Pushing my shorts down, my hard cock pops out as I run my finger along her snapper again.

"It's *cum*," I say to her as I push my cock against her soft labia. My manhood is buried into Lila quickly as I pull her hard toward me and begin to thrust.

"What are you doing?" my wife asks as she grips the edge of the tub tightly.

"Sharing with Sean, apparently," I grunt as I feel the unusual amount of moisture inside Lila's pussy. Though the thought of shoving my cock into my wife's hole for sloppy seconds is not the sort of thing that I would have seriously considered as recently as this morning, right now it seems to be the best thing to do. I am horny and I need to show in some way that Lila's twat is still *my* twat.

"I can't believe you would do that," Lila moans as she holds onto the tub. She lifts one hand to play with her clitoris as I pull hard on her hips. For some reason her soft, wet pouch feels incredibly sensual right now as I push as far as I can into her and feel her firm cervix at the end of her tunnel.

"Fuck, baby," I say to her as I bend over her and reach for her breasts. I pull gently on each one as I move faster and faster in and out of my wife. All the while, my brain thinks about how Sean's cock was inside her just a couple of hours before. "I'm glad you fucked him," I tell Lila as I move my fingers over her nipples. Her small body trembles as we each work ourselves up to a nice orgasm. When it finally happens, I am both surprised and amazed at the same time.

"Oh, BRANDON!!!" Lila squeaks loudly as I pound hard against her cervix. *"Ohhhhh...fuck...NAHHHH!!!"* She grinds her ass hard against me as she enjoys the sensation of my manhood buried deep inside her pussy. I can smell the sex from earlier on her as I thrust and wonder if Lila pressed her ass into Sean in exactly the same way. Oh, how I wish I could have watched them together earlier! It would have been the sort of experience I have always wanted to have with my wife in bed. The idea of her with another man has always been a sort of fantasy for me, and now I can see where that fantasy could become reality.

"Fuck!!!" The first volley of my semen rockets deep into her pussy against her cervix. *"Oh, SHIT!!!"* I release Lila's breasts and stand up so that I can grip her hips once again. Pulling hard on her, I thrust slowly as I empty my balls into her. *"Oh, honey...uhhh...mmmmm..."* Gritting my teeth, I run one of my hands along her lower back and her ass cheeks as

I enjoy feeling the inside of her soft, wet clapper. Lila has always been the best fuck for me, and I believe that more right now than I have ever before. She is the best at what she does, which is why Sean lost his wad with her.

After finishing up inside her, I pull out of my wife and step backward toward the countertop. My cock throbs as it drips some thick man gravy, it's length still undulating from what we have just finished doing. My eyes study Lila's sweet pecan as my own wet mix slowly rolls out of her hole and rehydrates her previous lover's dried semen.

"Brandon," she says quietly as she turns and sits down on the edge of the bathtub. "I'm sorry about today. It happened, but I didn't mean for it to."

I nod my head. "I know. He is a nice looking guy, huh?" I would smile, but I do not feel that such a thing would be completely appropriate given what has happened between us today. Though we have just had a quick bout of nice sex, there is still a very large snippet of truth between us. My wife fucked another man who had no clue that she was a married woman. It was my fault in a way, but even so I am having a hard time moving past the fact that Lila gave in so easily. I was there, after all. I was at the restaurant as they dined together and then she just walked right into the elevator with the other man to go to a room upstairs while I watched. Surely Lila knew that I would see her. How could I not?"

"What are we going to do now?" my wife finally asks as we quietly look at each other in the bathroom.

I shrug my shoulders. "I don't know. Things are really different right now for the both of us. Maybe we should take a shower and think it over?"

Lila smiles at me before turning and walking over to the shower. She leans in and turns on the water and waves me over to her. I pull off my shirt and kick my shorts away from my ankles before going to my beautiful wife. She makes me hard again as she reaches out and takes hold of my growing cock. Once again I will take the woman I married in this bathroom. It might take a few minutes for me to regain full-staff, but I will get there and we will both orgasm again. The idea that Sean and Lila had sex together this afternoon in the hotel is affecting us both in a very different way than I would have ever expected. It appears to be both of our intentions to seize upon that feeling.

Chapter Eight: Another Date

I have watched my wife for the last few days as her whole demeanor has changed. She has even passed up a couple of serious opportunities to take clients to view some very nice properties, instead passing off those potential commissions to other realtors in her office. This has set off a few alarm bells in my head as I think about what happened between her and Sean. Is the thought of him getting to her?

"Yes," Lila says to me after I ask whether she has been having thoughts of the young man from the show.

"And?" I press her. "What are you thinking?" My wife carefully lifts the cup of coffee she has been drinking while sitting on the terrace with me this morning.

Lila sighs. "I'm going to see him again, Brandon. I know that isn't something that you want to hear from me, but I don't know how else to say it. Sean and I are going to get together tomorrow evening at a hotel."

My heart skips a beat as I process this sudden revelation. "What do you mean by that, Lila? You're not going to go have *sex* with him again, are you?" I shake my head as I glare at her from my seat.

"It's something that I have to do," she tells me almost as if it is some sort of necessary treatment for a terrible medical condition. "I can't help that I want what I want."

"You can't *help* it?" Standing to my feet, I walk toward the edge of the terrace and look out over the city below. My mind races with all that I know about Lila's time with Sean at the hotel a few days ago. I heard what was happening through the door. It was sex; the kind that is dirty and hard. Though my wife tried for a time to convince me that it was nothing more than heavy petting or simply a little fun with their clothes on, she has recently been more open about what happened between her and the other man. Yes, she told me the other day, they had sex. She liked it and she even let Sean come inside her without a condom. The thrill of it is what pushed her to do it, even though she really did not know him at all. The thought of me being in the hotel was part of the excitement for her as well.

"Brandon, let's not argue," she tells me. "You and I both know that we have been having all sorts of fantasies about this sort of thing for a while. This is a good thing for our marriage, right? We can use this to move our sex life a little further along."

I chuckle as I run my hand over my head. "Where is this coming from? You normally don't talk like this, Lila. We have been married for ten years and our sex life has been pretty good so far. Now you're telling me that it's not all that great? That we need to move it along?"

"Just be open minded," she pleads. "Think about what this will do to help us get to know each other's sexual needs better..."

"*Open minded?* Our *sexual needs?* Are you listening to yourself, honey? Do you get what you're saying right now? You're talking about an open marriage arrangement, but we haven't come to that sort of agreement yet."

"*Yet,*" Lila says immediately with a smile. "You've been thinking about all of this too, haven't you? Brandon, be honest with me. Don't you actually *want* me to have sex with Sean so that I can tell you all about it later on?

"Dammit, Lila," I growl as I shake my head. "What you are asking for is over the top. You want to screw that guy when you shouldn't have even met him at all."

My wife narrows her eyes at me. "And whose fault is that?" She knows she has a point as she looks hard at me. It was my idea to bring her in on the television show and to use her to replace someone who did not show for the episode. I needed her and Lila came through in spades.

I sigh as I put a hand over my eyes. "I can't believe what you are asking of me, honey."

Lila walks up to me. "Come with me, Brandon. Let me have him and you can watch."

My cock becomes solid suddenly as I take my hand away and look at her. "*Watch?* Do you mean that you want me to watch you have sex with another man, Lila? That's really out of character for you. You don't even fantasize this way while we are having sex together."

She nods her head. "I know, sweetheart. Sometimes I tend to be a little less than giving in bed." I am stunned by the sudden admission by my spouse. Though we have a pretty good sex life, there are times when my wife is not exactly playful in bed. Sure, she is a great fuck every single time, but Lila will ignore me if I start talking a little about other people and how I am horny for someone else while penetrating her. No, talking dirty or even considering having sex with other people is not the sort of thing she has advocated over the last decade of marriage to me.

"You would let me watch you with Sean?" I ask as I try to decide whether the offer is some sort of attempt to catch me agreeing to something that I should not agree to. "This would go against everything we have said about our marriage in the past, honey. Don't toy with me if you are being serious."

Lila takes my hand and looks into my eyes. "I'm serious, Brandon. Come with me when I go meet him on Friday evening. You can be in the room if he's fine with it."

I shake my head. "Sean will probably not be okay with doing that sort of thing. Most men wouldn't want another man watching them having sex. Especially if we tell him that I am your husband."

"Don't tell him, then. You simply say that you are there for the sake of the dating show. Tell him that you want to be there so that you can tell the audience how things went." Lila's face turns a little red as she makes this offer to me. I feel my cock stiffen completely as I pre-come a little into my pants. The idea of seeing her fuck the other man makes me incredibly horny. I want to see them together in bed so badly.

Sighing, I tell her, "I'll have to make my presence there something that is realistic. Maybe I could say that I am filming everything for a special on HBO or something like that?"

"Sweetheart, I don't want a camera on me." My wife shakes her head as fear suddenly grips her. "Not while I'm having sex."

"It's fine, Lila," I tell her. "Look, I'll just use my cell phone. I'll tell him it's a point of view video that will give the audience a nice idea of just how much fun your time with each other is. Sean will go for that, I think." I am lying a little as I think about what I want to do. The young man seems very much into my wife, but being filmed might be a little too much for him. There was nothing in the interview process that would have let me know one way or the other about his thoughts on something so risqué.

"He can't know that we are married," Lila warns. "He might sell the story to a newspaper or do something even worse with that sort of information, Brandon. Neither of us can afford a scandal like that. My bosses at the real estate agency would feel as if I am no longer a good face for the agency. You can film us, but be discreet and stay back, alright?" Her body shivers. "I can't believe that we are talking about you watching me with Sean while getting it all on video. Will you be discreet, Brandon? Don't embarrass me, okay?" Her blue eyes look hard at me as she awaits my response.

"I would never intentionally do anything to embarrass you," I promise. "I love you too much, Lila. I will always love you no matter what."

"And I love you too, my sweet husband." She reaches up and pulls my head down to hers. Our lips touch and we kiss for a moment as Lila reaches toward the front of my pants and massages my swollen member just behind the thin material. My wife likes to play with me when we kiss passionately. Though she has another man in mind that she would like to share her body with, I am still her husband. That fact will not soon change even as she makes love to Sean.

Chapter Nine: Deep and Hard

61

Lila and I made our way up to the third floor of the same hotel where she met Sean more than a week ago. The hairs on the back of my neck stand up as I look around and recognize the lobby and the clerk's counter nearby. Though we do not have a camera following along, I do have my cell phone, fully charged, ready for filming. Thankfully, my wife called Sean and explained to him that the director of the show had called her and asked to be a part of any other meetings they had together. Lila was able to convince him that getting their sex on video would mean more exposure for both of them if it made it onto cable television. Surprisingly, he agreed that I should be there for the fun that would happen between them.

"I can't believe I'm going to watch my wife fuck another dude," I say with a laugh as the elevator doors close. Lila pushes the third floor button and looks over at me.

"Just play this cool, okay? Remember, he doesn't know that you are my husband, Brandon. Sean believes this will all lead to some sort of film deal later."

I shake my head. "I never took him for someone who wanted to be in film at all. I mean, aside from his desire to be on the program with three women."

"He seemed really into the idea of someone taking video of the two of us together," she replies. "Sean is a complex man, Brandon. If you spent some time getting to know him, you would see that his ideas on life are a little different than most other men."

"I have no doubt about that," I chuckle. "The problem is, I don't typically have the time to go on a dinner date with the men and women who come onto our show. They all seem really nice when they go through the interview process, but sometimes they aren't much company when they go on their dates." We have had more than a few young men and women who have been utter disappointments on their dates. This is the reason we do not always show the dates on television. Some are great for a viewing audience while others are boring or downright awful. Sean's date with Lila was very substantive, though.

"Just be nice, alright? No matter what happens, you have to stay back and just let things naturally progress. Don't be my husband tonight." Lila looks hard at me with her deeply blue eyes.

"I'll just film everything, my love. I promise."

"Remember, you don't know me all that well." We leave the elevator and make our way to room three-seventeen. Lila walks up to the door and knocks on it. In just moments the door opens and we see the young man standing on the other side of the threshold. "Hello, Sean." My wife walks forward and gives the man a kiss on the cheek. He smiles at her before looking at me.

"Hey, man. It's good to see you again." He reaches out and takes my hand to shake as I walk into the hotel room. Closing the door behind us, Sean motions toward the room and says, "Make yourselves comfortable." My body shakes a little as I walk toward the large king size bed. Seeing a chair available, I sit down and put one leg over the other as I try to relax. My heart is racing inside my chest as I watch the two of them together.

"This is a nice room," I comment while looking around. "You must have decided to drop a nice amount on it, Sean."

The young man nods his head. "You know, I loved it so much the last time that I thought I would come back here to get a room. It's all worth it when you consider the woman who has come to see me." He smiles at my wife as he takes her into his arms. They kiss hard this time, their lips locking tightly as their hands move along each others' bodies. There is passion between the two of them that I never thought I would see with Lila. Our marital bed, though given to plenty of sex, rarely sees the sort of deep passion that I am seeing just now between the both of them. It makes me jealous on the one hand, but then on the other I think about my own sexual fantasies.

"Are you fine if I film?" I ask as I pull my phone from my pocket.

"Dude, I don't care what you do. I just want a piece of this fine ass." Sean turns Lila around and pushes her against the bed. He slaps her ass and laughs as he runs his fingers along the hemline of her short skirt. I get hard as I begin to film the two of them together.

"Fuck, Sean," my wife laughs as she looks behind her. "You are getting a little rough early on, aren't you?"

"I'm horny," he tells her with a wicked grin on his face. "I have been wanting you all week long, baby." He pushes her skirt up and finds her lacey thong panties. Pulling it to one side, he quickly finds my wife's snapper and fingers it a little as his cock grows hard behind the material of his shorts.

"Oh, shit." Lila looks over at me as the young man fingers her snapper. She knows this is turning me on, but I get the feeling she is concerned that I might also become overly protective of her. She warned me that he would probably take her roughly. It is exactly the sort of thing he has said he wanted to do with her through text messages all week long. Sean is a horny man and he finds my wife incredibly sexy.

"You're already wet," he chuckles as he goes down on her. His hands push on Lila's ass, causing her to drop her head to the bed. Sean laps at her wet labia as he tastes of her sweet sap. I get up from my chair and walk over to be closer to them and to get the young man's tongue on video. He flicks my wife's swollen clitoris over and over again with his tongue as he tastes of her. Oh, how I want to be a part of what is going on right now between the two of them.

"Stop," Lila says as she turns around. Sean pulls back from her and watches as she lies back on the bed and begins to unbutton her blouse. It takes only a minute or so for her to remove her top and her bra, along with her other clothes, before opening her legs for the young man. He smiles as he goes down on her again and pushes her legs back with his hands.

"Good stuff," I mutter as I zoom in on my wife's wet pussy. Sean obviously loves to taste of her as she butters up for him. My cock is hard and pre-coming now as I watch this all take place.

"I need you," Sean tells her as he lifts up from her muff and moves her petite body around on the bed. He pulls her toward him and buries his large stalk deep into her waiting pussy. Lila shudders a little as he stretches her vagina like a glove around his erect phallus. Well-endowed, Sean begins to thrust in and out of my wife's soft hole, her toes pointing hard as he finds her cervix and forces the end of his cock against it.

"Oh, fuck," Lila moans as she plays with her own nipples. "Sean, you fucking sexy man." She giggles a little as he fucks her hard, my wife's feet now on top of his shoulders as Sean penetrates her deeply. The young man thrusts in and out of her as his balls slap her puckered asshole each time. I make sure to get all of this on video as I walk around the two of them. I am amazed that so far neither of them have noticed that I am hard and wetting down the front of my pants. Though I am horny, I would prefer that I could keep that a secret from the two of them. Much more pre-coming on my part would likely inform the two of them of the way I feel at this moment.

"Shit, baby," Sean moans as his face turns deep red. "You are a tight little thing." I watch as my wife grinds her pelvis hard against her lover. "I'm going to come inside you, Lila. I hope you're ready for me."

My wife's face turns red. *"HOLY FUCK!!!"* Her small body bucks hard beneath Sean as she suddenly begins to orgasm. *"Motherfucker...MOTHERFUCKER!!!"* If she were not my wife I would probably laugh at the way she is reacting to how Sean is fucking her. However, I know Lila very well. When she comes this hard she is very much horny and very much in need of release. *"Ohhhh...OHHHHHH!!!"* I continue to film closely to the two lovers as I move the camera from my wife's pussy to her face. She seems to no longer be aware that I am in the room with them as she releases during her orgasm.

"Baby..." Sean pushes her legs further back. *"Oh, fuck...baby...BABY...UHHH...UHHH...OHHHHHH..."* He comes hard inside her tight snapper as he releases the bounty of his balls deep inside her womb. The volume of his thick, white man gravy must be large as I watch some of it begin to erupt from Lila's pussy from around his solid man meat. *"Uhhh...fuck...ohhhh..."* The two of them come hard together as they finish their orgasms. Lila is the first to relax as the young man finishes his fun inside her. I am certain to capture every single part of their time together as I lick my lips and think about what it would be to have sex with my wife now that Sean's spunk is inside her.

"You are a naughty boy," Lila laughs as she pulls the young man down to her. They kiss passionately for some time before Sean pulls his manhood out of her and moves to where my wife's head is lying on a pillow. He says nothing as she reaches out with a hand and guides his wilting johnson to her mouth. She begins to clean his pecker with her lips and tongue as the young man brushes her hair from her face.

"Thank you," he replies as I finish filming and put my cell phone away. I have gotten what I wanted at this point.

"That was pretty intense," I tell the two of them. "You must be really into each other."

Sean looks at her and nods his head. "I guess so. It's just all fun, right? Life's short, so live it hard." He smiles at me before reaching for the table by the bed and picking up a pack of cigarettes.

"Wait, you smoke?" I say while shaking my head.

"Well, yeah." Sean lights a cigarette as he holds it in his mouth and takes a quick drag from it. "Started again after I met Lila. I don't know, I guess she just reminded me of all that I had given up when I left college. Having a nice cigarette after sex is the ultimate cap to good sex, you know what I mean?" He smiles at me as I nod my head. Lila and I would never consider smoking for ourselves, though we frequently imbibe in a little alcohol now and again.

"You are always fun, sweetie." Lila stands up from the bed and goes to where he is standing. They kiss again, hard and with a great deal of passion, as I watch them together.

"Hey, will you give us some private time?" Sean asks as he looks at me and motions toward the hotel room door with his head. Though I want to tell him that Lila is with me, I do not want to tip him off as to the true identity of my wife. Besides, I promised her that I would keep that quiet, and I will. That does not mean that I will think good things about the young lover.

"Yeah, I'll leave now. Thanks for the footage."

"Our pleasure." Sean allows a wicked smile before he turns to Lila once again to kiss her. It takes a lot within me to walk away from the hotel room while knowing that my wife remains behind, but I do so anyway. I have seen what they do together, and that is worth letting them have a little fun out of my sight.

"I hope you aren't too serious about him," I say quietly to myself as I imagine talking to Lila. "I hope you are still mine." I make my way to the elevator so that I can go to the lobby and then leave the hotel. Lila will be out soon and we can talk then.

Chapter Ten: A Quiet Understanding

"You know that I could add a lot of fun to that show, Brandon," Lila says with an annoying giggle as we walk along the sidewalk in front of several shops in Hollywood. Though we rarely actually buy things here, we cannot help but enjoy looking at the things they have on sale sitting in the windows.

"No," I reply flatly as I shake my head. "Stop asking me to let you appear on the show again, honey." It was funny the first few times when my wife requested being put back on the show once again, but it has become a bit irritating as I realize she is somewhat serious about the suggestion. "If someone were to recognize you the second time around, we would both get into some serious trouble."

"That's the fun of it, though, right?" It has been years since I have seen Lila so excited about doing something so daring. Her time with Sean has come to an end, with both of them tiring of each other and wanting to seek other lovers for now.

"I don't want to lose this gig," I tell her. "I'm finally doing very well for myself and you also have your real estate career to consider. We don't need to make things hard on ourselves, my love."

Lila looks at my crotch. "Oh, I think I've been making things hard for you for a while now." She winks one of her blue eyes at me as she walks up to one of the shop windows. "That dress is so slutty, Brandon. Maybe you should get it for me."

"What?" I shake my head as I look at the expensive cocktail dress. "Why would you want that dress? You have lots of nice dresses at home, including three or four cocktail dresses." I smile at the beautiful woman in front of me and ask, "What will it take to get you to cool down on all this, my love? What is it that you *really* want?"

My wife walks up to me and gives me a quick kiss on the lips before telling me, "I want to find another man, Brandon. I want to do it again."

"Shit, Lila," I say quietly as she grabs the bulge in my pants. "Not here." I look around at the other people walking past us on the sidewalk.

The fact is, many of them have seen much crazier behavior on the streets of Hollywood, so this is not something that is likely to shock them.

"You like it when I touch you, don't you?" Lila smiles wickedly at me. "You have lists of other guys for the show, right? Find one for me, Brandon. Tell him that you are filming a television show for some other channel and that you want to film me with him. Just like you did with Sean."

"Fuck," I whimper quietly as I realize that I have created a bit of a monster. "Are you serious?"

"*Very* serious," she replies. "Give me another one, alright? Do this for me and I swear sex for you will be ten times better in the future." Lila seems to be on a sort of sexual high at the moment as she looks into my eyes. I cannot believe how much she wants this. The fact is, I want it almost as much as she does.

"Okay," I answer. "What if I could get someone? Are you thinking about doing a lot of the same stuff as you did with Sean?

"Maybe," she replies. "But I want to get kinkier, Brandon. I want to do things with another man that will *shock* him. Buy me one of those harnesses that hang from the ceiling and he can fuck me like that." Lila giggles as she moves in to give me another kiss. This time, we spend a while embracing and trading tongues as people continue to walk by on the sidewalk. My cock hard, I begin to pre-come a lot into my underwear and I realize that a wet spot is probably appearing right now on the front of my pants. Lila is so hot now that she has become loosened up and open to what can happen between her and another man. It makes me horny as I consider all the possibilities.

"So, I'll find a guy and you'll have sex with him," I say into her ear. "Will you fuck me at the same time? Maybe a threesome thing?"

Lila smiles. "Maybe, my love. Let's take just one thing at a time, okay?"

"Yeah, okay." We kiss a moment longer before my wife takes my hand and leads me along the sidewalk once more.

"You're having fun today, aren't you?" she observes as she looks at my crotch once more.

"Yeah, and everyone will know about it," I laugh. We both continue to make our way along the shops in Hollywood, occasionally stopping to kiss and talk about what Lila wants to do now that Sean is no longer her other lover. There is a list in a file drawer in my office right now with about forty names and phone numbers of men waiting to get onto the dating show. This afternoon I will go there and begin considering all of the applicants for a special appearance with my wife. Maybe we will find a young man so into Lila that he will take her even further in her sexual desires than Sean could have ever done. I am not sure that I will find such a man, but I intend to at least try. I want to see my wife with someone else once again and then fuck her hard while thinking about how it turned her on. Soon she shall have her sexy lover. And after that, she will have me.

THE END

Don't miss out!

Visit the website below and you can sign up to receive emails whenever Karly Violet publishes a new book. There's no charge and no obligation.

https://books2read.com/r/B-A-GIXE-SDKJB

BOOKS 2 READ

Connecting independent readers to independent writers.

Did you love *Hotwife Blind Date - A Steamy Romance Hot Wife Novel*?
Then you should read *Hotwife And The Boyfriend From The Past - A
Wife Watching Hotwife Romance Novel*[1] by Karly Violet!

***Would you let your wife fall back into the arms of her virile and sexually
adventurous ex-boyfriend?***

Russ can't believe his eyes as he stares back at his wife's
phone.**Naughty messages exchanged between her and her
ex-boyfriend taunts his masculinity.**The perplexed husband confronts
Tony and demands an explanation.Why, after several years of marriage
and a sexually adventurous life, does his beautiful wife feel the need
to exchange explicit messages with her ex-boyfriend?And not just any
ex, but one that the loyal husband feels threatened by .Tonya confesses
that she misses the **sweaty non-stop bedroom action she experienced**

---

1. https://books2read.com/u/bWPBx0

2. https://books2read.com/u/bWPBx0

nightly with her past boyfriend. And longed for it for just one more night .Russ's immediate emotions should have confusion, anger and jealousy.But they weren'tStrangely, **the thought of his wife with another man** piqued his interest and aroused a hidden fantasy of his.

Can a stable marriage handle the inclusion of a wife's more experienced and passionate lover from her past?

'Hotwife And The Boyfriend From The Past' is part 1 of the 3 part series Hot Wife Shared and explores the start of a Hotwife journey a couple take as they introduce a virile young ex boyfriend back into the stunning wife's life.

Read more at https://www.patreon.com/karlyviolet.

About the Author

Sign up to my mailing list to receive the two free epilogues for 'A Hotwife Adventure' and 'Hotwife Training' and to stay up to date on all of my latest releases! http://eepurl.com/c3ICWf Sign up to my Patreon account and receive exclusive Hotwife stories every month and sexy scenes every week! https://www.patreon.com/karlyviolet

Read more at https://www.patreon.com/karlyviolet.

About the Publisher